Have I Got DOGS!

Have I Got

DOGS!

By William Cole

Illustrated by Margot Apple

PUFFIN BOOKS

PUFFIN BOOKS
Published by the Penguin Group
Penguin Books USA Inc.,
375 Hudson Street, New York, New York 10014, U.S.A.
Penguin Books Ltd, 27 Wrights Lane, London W8 5TZ, England
Penguin Books Australia Ltd, Ringwood, Victoria, Australia
Penguin Books Canada Ltd, 10 Alcorn Avenue,
Toronto, Ontario, Canada M4V 3B2
Penguin Books (N.Z.) Ltd, 182–190 Wairau Road,
Auckland 10, New Zealand
Penguin Books Ltd, Registered Offices:
Harmondsworth, Middlesex, England

First published in the United States of America by
Viking, a division of Penguin Books USA Inc., 1993
Published in Puffin Books, 1996

1 2 3 4 5 6 7 8 9 10

THE LIBRARY OF CONGRESS HAS CATALOGED THE VIKING EDITION AS FOLLOWS:
Cole, William, Have I got dogs!/William Cole;
illustrated by Margot Apple.   p. cm.
Summary: The owner of all kinds of dogs describes,
in rhyme, the unique features of each.
ISBN 0-670-83070-4
[1. Dogs—Fiction. 2. Stories in rhyme.]
I. Apple, Margot, ill. II. Title.
PZ8.3.C675Hav   1993 [E]—dc20   93-12464   CIP AC

Puffin Books ISBN 0-14-054195-0

Printed in the U.S.A.

For George Booth . . . my hero.

—M.A.

Have I got dogs, pedigreed and mutts—
I've got so many, people think I'm nuts!

See my dalmatian? Her name is Dot.
She's an easy dog to spot.

My Irish wolfhound's as tall as a pony.
She's so skinny that I named her Bony.

My Pom's the tiniest of all my gang.
I was just being funny when I named him Fang!

There's the schnauzer—I call him Snappy.
He sure doesn't make the postman happy!

Look at my curly-tailed, flat-faced pug.
He looks so funny I named him Mug.

The prettiest dog of all, by golly,
is lovely Lassie—of *course* she's a collie!

Now here's a fellow with hustle and bustle:
the little terrier called Jack Russell.

Needle-nose is my speedy whippet.
Wanna race her? No thanks—skip it!

My old dachshund is a bit of a crank.
He looks like a hot dog so I call him Frank.

Tiny, the Chihuahua, is easy to pick up.
And when she barks it's like a hiccup!

Look at my red-haired Irish setter.
I named him Rusty (but I could do better).

Oh, there's the clumsiest of all my mutts.
I had no choice but to call him Klutz!

Did you ever see such a handsome poodle?
She's kind of silly so I named her Noodle.

My English bulldog looks quite tough.
But he's short-tempered, that's why he's Gruff.

There's Flop, the long-eared basset hound.
She makes a scary baying sound!

When mealtime comes, I give a call,
and you should see the free-for-all!